Based on a true story . . .

Seven year old Jack has autism. Bear was his companion, and a bridge to the world around him. When Bear went missing, Jack's dad sent out a tweet that went viral as his son's story touched the hearts of people around the globe.

Dawn Coulter-Cruttenden's beautiful picture book shows how the kindness of strangers helped Jack slowly come to terms with the bear-shaped hole in his life.

Please Have you seen my bear and could you bring it back to Jack. is you find it Thank you

For Martha, Gracie, Hal and Sue . . .
but especially for Jack.

OXFORD
UNIVERSITY PRESS

Great Clarendon Street,
Oxford OX2 6DP

Oxford University Press
is a department of the University of Oxford.
It furthers the University's objective of excellence
in research, scholarship,and education by publishing
worldwide. Oxford is a registered trade mark
of Oxford University Press in the UK
and in certain other countries

Text and illustration copyright
© Dawn Coulter-Cruttenden 2020

The moral rights of
the author and illustrator
have been asserted
Database right Oxford University
Press (maker)

First published 2020

British Library Cataloguing in Publication Data
Data available

ISBN: 978-0-19-277211-4

1 3 5 7 9 10 8 6 4 2

Printed in China

Paper used in the production of this book is a natural,
recyclable product made from wood grown in sustainable forests.
The manufacturing process conforms to the environmental
regulations of the country of origin.

Bear Shaped

Dawn Coulter-Cruttenden

OXFORD
UNIVERSITY PRESS

Jack and Bear were best friends.
They did everything together.
They went everywhere together.

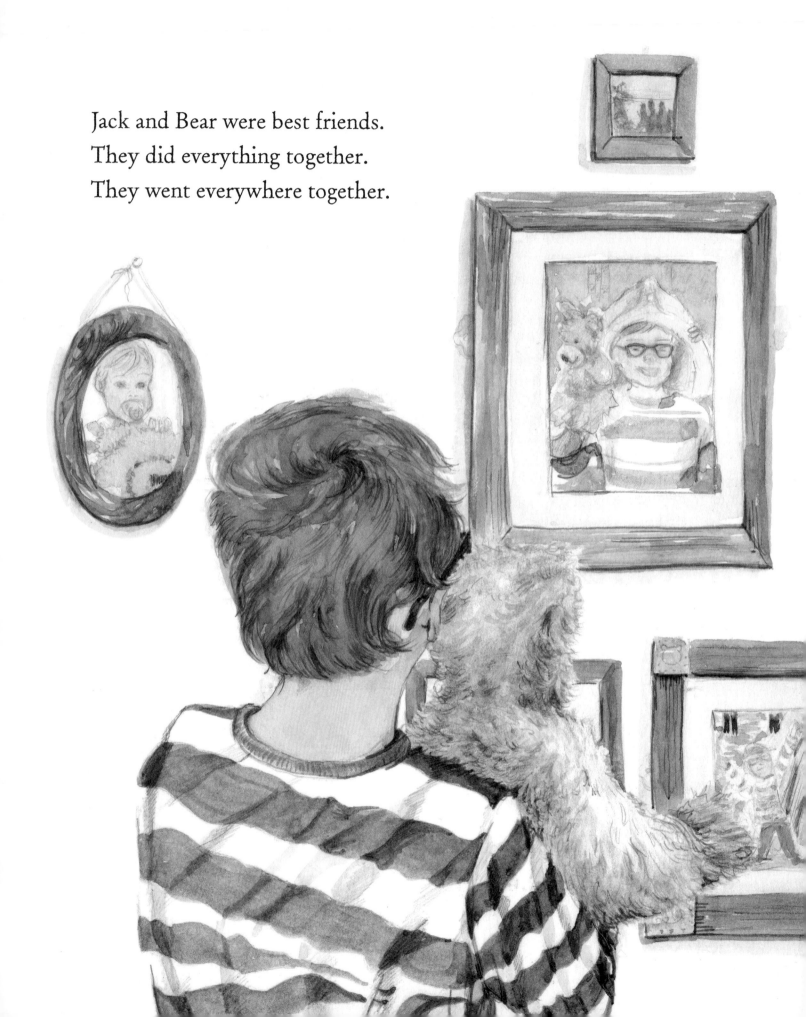

Jack carried Bear in his schoolbag.

He carried him in his rucksack.

And he carried
him in his arms.

Bear was special because
he made Jack feel **brave**.

Sometimes when people
spoke to Jack, he felt too shy
to even **look** at them.

So he would hold Bear in
front of his face and talk
through him.

**Bear was fine
with that.**

Sometimes, when Jack was **nervous** about trying something new,

Bear would try it first so Jack knew it would be okay.

Bear was fine with that tooooooooooo.

When Jack wanted to be away from people and noise,
he and Bear would make a secret den for their own quiet time.

They would read
together, **snuggle**
together, and just be.

At bedtime, Jack would show Bear how to join the stars
to make pictures—like dot-to-dot puzzles in the sky.

Bear thought Jack was very clever indeed.

He really wasn't like any
other Jack in the world.
He was **Bear's** Jack.

Over time, all the love, cuddles, and adventures that Jack shared with him made Bear's fur beautifully shaggy and soft.

He really wasn't like any other bear in the world.
He was **Jack's** Bear.

One morning, Jack and
Bear got up early . . .

. . . and spent the whole
day at the park.

And sometime in the middle of
that very special day . . .

. . . Bear disappeared.

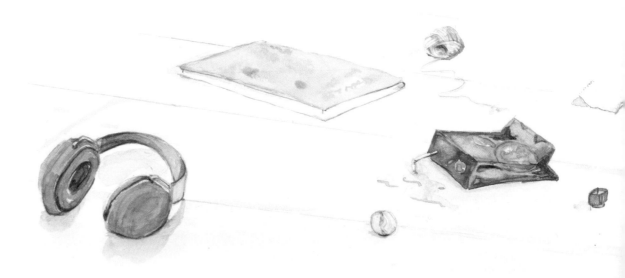

Jack didn't know **when** exactly.

Or **how** exactly.

Or **where** exactly . . .

Bear was just . . . GONE.

Jack felt a big Bear-shaped hole
opening up inside him. It was a sore,
sad, empty kind of a hole.

Jack didn't like it.

In the mornings, Jack would wake up and for a few
seconds the hole wouldn't be there. Then he would look
at where Bear used to sleep and remember:

Bear was gone.

And the hole would come back.

Jack missed Bear so much
that he kept thinking
he saw him.

It was as if Bear was **everywhere** and
nowhere at the same time.

Jack's mum and dad asked everyone
they knew to look out for Bear.
They even asked people they didn't
know: complete strangers!

Meanwhile, Jack decided
to make posters.

He put them **everywhere**.

He hoped somebody
would find Bear and
send him home.

But nobody did.

One morning, something special began to happen.

A bear-shaped parcel arrived in the post.

Inside was a big, fluffy bear.
It was a **lovely** bear . . .
. . . but it wasn't Bear.

The next day, **another** bear arrived.

The day after that,
another one.

Then **another**. . .
and **another** . . . and
another . . .

Messages began to arrive too. From all over the world.
People sent letters, and notes, and pictures of their own
bears. They sent old bears. They sent new bears.

All the strangers who'd heard about Bear had talked to other strangers . . .

. . . who had talked to other strangers . . .

. . . who had talked to other strangers . . .

. . . until hundreds and hundreds
of people were looking out for Bear.

Somehow, they all understood how Jack felt.
Many of them had known that empty sad space too.

Over time
every little bit
of kindness began to
soften the edges of the
**bear-shaped
hole.**

Slowly,
Jack began
to realise that he was
very lucky to have had
a friend like Bear.
He began to smile again
remembering all their
adventures, their secrets,
and their hugs.

Then, Jack had a sad thought.
But this time, not for himself.
And not for Bear.

He thought of all the people who had never
known a bear like Bear. He thought of all the
people who had lost a friend like Bear.
And Jack made a **big, brave,**
bear-shaped decision . . .

He gave all the new bears away.

He knew there were other children who
needed something special to make them
feel brave when they needed to.

A bear to share
hugs and to make
memories with.

Jack understood now, that although
Bear was gone from his side, he had
known so much love that he would
always be with him.

It's true that he couldn't carry
him in his schoolbag.

He couldn't carry him
in his rucksack.

And he couldn't carry
him in his arms.

But he would **always**
carry him in his heart . . .

... like a bear-shaped smile.